You and Your Pet
Guinea Pig

Jean Coppendale

QEB Publishing

QEB Publishing, Inc.
23062 La Cadena Drive
Laguna Hills
Irvine
CA 92653

Library of Congress Control Number: 2004101761

ISBN 1-59566-052-6

Written by Jean Coppendale
Consultant: Michaela Miller
Designed by Susi Martin
Editor: Gill Munton
All photographs by Jane Burton except
fruit on pages 20 and 21 by Chris Taylor
With many thanks to Melissa and Roy Payne
Picture of Squeaker on page 29 by Georgie Meek

Creative Director: Louise Morley
Editorial Manager: Jean Coppendale

Printed and bound in China

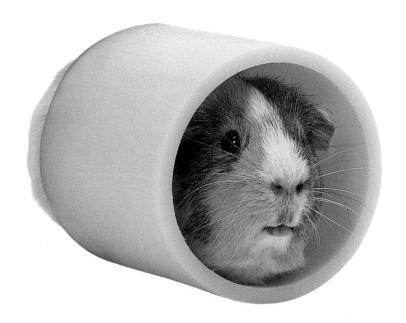

Words in **bold** are
explained on page 32.

Contents

Your first guinea pig

Guinea pigs can make lovely pets. Once they get to know you, they like to be petted and held gently. But guinea pigs are not toys. They are small and fragile, and easily hurt. They also need a lot of looking after, because they must be kept clean and well fed.

▲ **Guinea pigs like to play outside.**

▶ **Guinea pigs can live for up to seven years.**

▼ **The proper name for a guinea pig is a cavy.**

Guinea pigs are fun and like to explore

▶ **Guinea pigs may seem timid at first, but they soon relax and play.**

Lots of guinea pigs

Guinea pigs are all the same shape but have different markings and colorings.

◀ **Some guinea pigs, such as this red Agouti, are all one color.**

▼ **These Alpaca guinea pigs have long, silky coats.**

► This guinea pig has a big white stripe.

◄ This gray and white guinea pig has rosetted fur.

▼ This crested Sheltie guinea pig has long hair.

Which guinea pig?

Guinea pigs like to live in groups, so you should buy at least two. Buy two boys or two girls from the same **litter**.

Guinea pigs have long and short hair. A long-haired guinea pig will need to be brushed every day but all guinea pigs will enjoy being brushed.

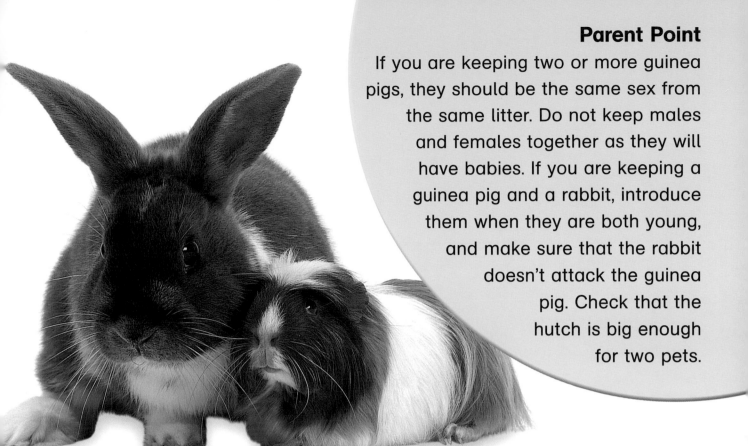

Parent Point
If you are keeping two or more guinea pigs, they should be the same sex from the same litter. Do not keep males and females together as they will have babies. If you are keeping a guinea pig and a rabbit, introduce them when they are both young, and make sure that the rabbit doesn't attack the guinea pig. Check that the hutch is big enough for two pets.

Guinea pigs usually get on with rabbits, so you can keep a rabbit with your guinea pig to stop it getting lonely. But the two pets should be brought up together. Always keep a check on them to make sure the rabbit does not bully the guinea pig.

▲ **A guinea pig and a rabbit can be good friends.**

▶ **Short-haired guinea pigs are easier to look after.**

9

Guinea pig shopping list

Your guinea pig will need

▶ **An indoor hutch**

▼ **An outdoor run**

◀ **Wood shavings**

▶ **Two water bottles, one for the hutch and one for the run, and a bottle brush**

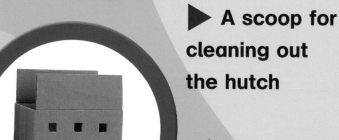

◀ **Hay for the bedding**

▶ **A scoop for cleaning out the hutch**

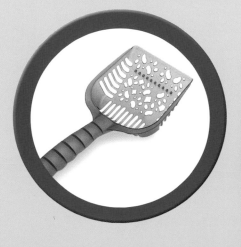

◀ **A carrier for trips to the vet**

◀ A gnawing block is needed to help teeth and gums stay healthy

▶ Two heavy food bowls, one for the hutch and one for the run

▲ Guinea pig food

Getting ready

Place the hutch in a warm, quiet spot if it is indoors. The hutch should have a closed-off area so that the guinea pig has a private place to sleep. The main part of the hutch should have an open wire grid front, so that the guinea pig can look out.

Put a layer of old newspaper on the floor of the hutch. Spread lots of wood shavings (but not cedar or pine) on top of the newspaper. Put a layer of hay on top of this. Make sure there is lots of hay in the sleeping area for the guinea pigs to make a cozy nest.

Your guinea pig should have a run (or another hutch) in the garden so that it can go outside in the summer. The run should be sturdy so that it cannot be accidentally knocked over. Always bring your guinea pig indoors at night.

Saying hello

When your guinea pigs arrive, they may
be feeling very scared. Place them gently
in their hutch, and leave them alone for
a little while so that they can get used
to their new home.

Always approach your guinea pig from the front, not the side. Talk quietly to your pet—loud noises and shouting will scare it.

▲ **Make sure your pets have fresh food to eat.**

Parent Points
Make sure your child knows how to handle the guinea pig before he or she tries to pick it up (see pages 16–17).

Handle with care

Make sure your guinea pig is used to you before you pick it up. Start by petting it gently with one finger while it is eating, then use your hand. Don't pick up your guinea pig unless you are sitting or kneeling down. To pick it up, put one hand under its rear end and the other round its shoulders. Let your guinea pig sit in your cupped hands. If it starts to squirm or squeal, gently put it back in its hutch. Never put the guinea pig on a table or chair, as it may fall off and hurt itself.

▶ **Talk gently to a timid guinea pig.**

Make sure the guinea pig is not left alone in a room when it is out of its hutch, as it may hurt itself, or damage furniture by chewing it.

Your child should never run round while holding the guinea pig. If the guinea pig does have a fall, put it back in the hutch. Check that it is eating and moving about as normal. If it appears dazed or in pain, or if you are not sure, call your local vet for advice immediately.

▼ **Never squeeze or drop your pet.**

Looking after your guinea pigs

If your guinea pig has short hair, brush it once a week. If it has long hair, it will need brushing every day. Brush the fur in the same direction as it grows, and don't press hard.

▲ A guinea pig's teeth are growing all the time. Give your pet a block of wood to gnaw. This will keep its teeth short and sharp.

▲ Make sure your guinea pig always has plenty of fresh water and food.

◀ **Brush your pet with a soft baby brush. Put a towel on your lap to catch the fur.**

Feeding your guinea pigs

Your guinea pigs should have two meals a day. Buy special guinea pig food from a pet store. Make sure your guinea pigs always have clean food.

Guinea pig food

Kale

Chicory

Apple

Your guinea pigs will enjoy being fed treats, such as a slice of apple and carrot sticks, and other pieces of fresh fruit and vegetables. Always wash fresh foods before you feed them to your pets.

Carrot

Cauliflower

Parent Points
Make sure the guinea pig isn't given too much lettuce or cabbage. Vitamin C is important to keep your guinea pigs healthy—check with your vet. Never feed them raw greens or green beans.

Keep it clean

Your guinea pigs' hutch needs to be kept clean. Once a day, use the scoop to clear out any droppings and dirty hay, and to remove any old bits of food. Put in some fresh hay. Wash the food bowls. Clean the water bottle with a special brush.

Once a month, give the hutch a really good clean. Throw away all the old newspaper, wood shavings and hay. Wipe the hutch down with disinfectant and water. When the hutch is dry, put in fresh newspaper, wood shavings, and hay.

Always wash your hands after you have cleaned the hutch.

◀ **While you are cleaning the hutch, keep your guinea pigs in a box, their exercise area, or the outdoor run.**

▶ **Don't forget to clean your pet's bowls.**

▼ **Once a week change the bedding completely. Throw away the old bedding and put in new, clean bedding.**

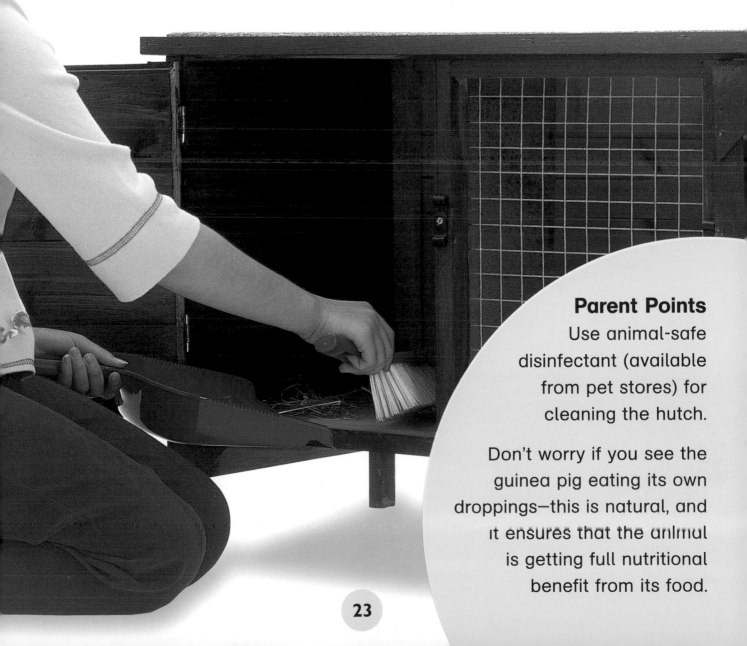

Parent Points
Use animal-safe disinfectant (available from pet stores) for cleaning the hutch.

Don't worry if you see the guinea pig eating its own droppings—this is natural, and it ensures that the animal is getting full nutritional benefit from its food.

Your guinea pig's life cycle

▼ At about five weeks, a female guinea pig can have babies of her own.

③

◀ **A newborn guinea pig has hair, and can see and walk.**

▲ **Guinea pigs suckle or drink their mother's milk until they are 3–4 weeks old.**

1

2

Let's explore!

Guinea pigs do not play with toys, but they need lots of exercise and like to explore. You can make an exciting indoor guinea pig play area in an old drawer. Inside the drawer put some old cardboard boxes and open-ended plastic tubes. Cut holes in the boxes for your pets to crawl through. Or put the boxes and the tubes on the floor so you can see the fun close up.

▼ **Young adult guinea pigs enjoy running through plastic tubes and exploring boxes.**

If your child is playing with the guinea pig in the yard, make sure that the area is safe. The guinea pig must not be able to escape, and you should check that no cats or dogs are nearby.

Guinea pigs can become sunburned. If yours is playing outside, make sure it is in the shade.

Saying goodbye

As your guinea pig grows older, it will spend more and more time sleeping. This is normal. Make sure it is warm and cozy, and that it feels safe and secure.

If your pet is very old or ill, it may die. Try not to be too sad, but remember all the fun you had together. You may want to bury your pet in the yard.

▼ **When your guinea pig is awake, pet it gently. If it is breathing strangely, tell an adult.**

Squeaker last sum

My pet Squeaker

Remember all the fun you had together

Guinea pig checklist

Read this list, and think about all the points.

✔ Guinea pigs are not toys.

✔ How will you treat your guinea pig if it makes you angry?

✔ Animals feel pain, just as you do.

✔ Treat your guinea pig gently—as you would like to be treated yourself.

✔ Most guinea pigs live for about seven years—will you get bored with your pet?

✔ Will you be happy to clean out your pet's hutch every day?

✔ Never hit your pet, shout at it, drop it, or throw things at it.